Escape From Email HELL

10 Email Edicts You Need To Know

By Craig Huggart

Printed in the United States of America

Edition 1.0

ISBN: 978-1-4357-0349-0

Table of Contents

Money back guarantee

Read this book and apply the proven principles it delivers. If you don't feel it was worth the money, I will refund the purchase price in full. Just contact me, no questions asked. To find my current contact information, visit http://www.craighuggart.com/ and check my LinkedIn information.

Forward *by Lisa Haneberg*

All of my clients - 100% - have asked me to help them tame their email mess. I am going to give them all a copy of this book - it's that good. Craig Huggart is a master email blaster and he can help anyone get out of email hell with a smile on their face!

Are you CCd, BCCd, and FYI'd to death? Do you want to scream each Monday morning when you see several hundred new emails clogging your inbox? Fight back. Escape from Email Hell will show you how.

Lisa Haneberg, writer and business consultant, Haneberg Management

Disclaimer

While I firmly believe applying these principles will transform your work life and free you from Email Hell, there is always the possibility that doing so could lead to you being fired from your job, your spouse getting mad at you or worse. Please use common sense and don't be stupid. In other words, apply what is said with caution and if it backfires on you, don't sue me.

Thanks

To my wonderful wife and my great kids for putting up with me while I worked on this book.

To my Mom and Dad, thanks for always believing in me and being my cheerleaders.

To the great folks who reviewed my drafts: John Winstanley, Andrew S. Rogers, Alan L. Plastow, MAT, PMP, and Frank T. You made the book so much better.

To the people (listed below) who gave me the information and inspiration to develop this system. I highly recommend their work.

- David Allen's Getting Things DONE

- Michael Linenberger's Total Workday Control

- Sally McGhee's Take Back Your Life

- Merlin Mann's www.43folders.com

- Timothy Ferriss' 4-Hour Workweek

Introduction

What is the most important skill in the workplace today? For a majority, it's how you manage your email.

Disagree? Would you say it's in the top 10?

Why read the book? You will find ideas that will decrease the amount of time it takes and the amount of stress it generates to manage your emails. And besides, the book is short and entertaining (I hope). Beyond that, it is my hope that you will discover a comprehensive system that can be applied to whatever email package you use.

How to get the most out of the book? Read one chapter at a time and apply that chapter until it becomes a habit. How long will that take? I'm guessing between one week and one month. How long until you notice a significant difference? Around six months. I have arranged the chapters in a logical order but feel free to skip to the ones that are most relevant to you.

Why is email a problem? According to 2006 numbers, the average information worker (that's you) gets over 20,000 messages per year. If you deal with 95% of your messages well, you end up with 1,000 messages in your Inbox. So, with email, your efficiency grade of 95% is a big fat F.

And . . . it's going to get worse. Some experts see Google as typifying the workplace of the future. Many people at Google get 500 messages per day. One person gets over 800 per day.

If you don't become *super hero good* at managing your email, it is going to overwhelm you.

But . . .

This is not one of those books that consumes time having it's pages convincing you of a problem. Most people, if they were honest with themselves, would admit that they are already well aware of how much of their lives are consumed in Email Hell.

So what are you waiting for . . . turn the page!

Chapter 1

Are you in Email Hell? Know someone who is? Keep reading.

You know Ed. He's a middle-aged man in a middle-sized company who gets tons of email. Whether you are drowning in email or skillfully riding the wave, you'll find something in his story that takes a little stress out of your email. So let's join Ed on a typical Wednesday afternoon.

It was a dark and stormy night . . . Oh, wait; that's just the "music" on my iPod. I'm sitting here in a cubicle that's so small I can't spin my chair around without hitting something. At times, even with my earbuds in, I can hear three or four simultaneous conversations going on around me. People even check their voice-mail by putting it on speaker. The nerve!

But that's not the worst of it. Oh, my God, I just opened my Inbox and found I have gone over the 4000 messages mark. It grows every day. I've tried and tried but nothing seems to work. I think I may need to quit this job just so I can get my email under control. And it's not much better at home. With 5 personal addresses, just checking them is a pain. And half of the messages are just JUNK! This whole email thing has got me stressed out. I sincerely want to slap the guy that invented it.

That night, after Ed goes to sleep . . .

I'm drowning . . . Can't get my breath . . . Waves are crashing over me again and again . . . I'm sinking in an endless sea of emails . . . God help me!

And an angel appears.

Who are you?

You don't need to know my given name. Call me "The email angel".

Where am I?

You are in Email Hell.

Hell?

That's right. You are stuck in an endless pattern where your email load gets greater and greater with each passing day. If you don't do something, it will kill you.

Kill me?!

Yes. The constant stress will eventually give you a heart attack. You will die at your desk, Ed, years before you're eligible to begin that fantasy retirement you keep dreaming about...

But I've tried and tried and tried and nothing works.

*Do not fear, that's why I'm here. I have been sent to help you escape from Email Hell. Understand, I can show you the way but **you** must follow the path.*

The Email Angel hands Ed a business card.

And the card said . . .

Declare Email Emancipation Day

Move all the email in your Inbox to a folder called Freedom.
Send an email to everyone and tell them what you've done.

Then the angel said, "You cannot use the card more than once a
year without endangering your reputation". The dream ended and
Ed woke up feeling like he had a new lease on life.

So what about you? Do you need to declare Email Emancipation
Day? Do you ever feel like you're in Email Hell? If so, try it: Declare
Email Emancipation Day.

Here is Ed's email to help get you started. Feel free to use all or
part of it.

> *Dear All:*
>
> *Because of the volume of emails I receive and my bad habits in managing them, my Inbox was too full. So, I have taken a bold step in managing them. I deleted all the emails from my Inbox. If you had previously sent me an email about something, something that you honestly need me to respond to, please resend it.*
>
> *Thanks,*
>
> *Ed*

For some this is the only way out. Not everyone needs to do this but those of you who do know who you are. It's simply too distracting to try and change your habits with thousands of messages in your Inbox. Once you set some good habits in place you may want to revisit your "Freedom" folder (or not). Just like other forms of communication, emails have a shelf life. When they get too stale, they are pretty much worthless. So why not try it. You're not going to read all those emails anyway. This is a great step not only for you but to the authors of all those emails. It's going to feel great looking at that empty Inbox.

For those who can take a less drastic approach, I suggest setting aside several hours or even a day to just focus on email. Keep working at it until your Inbox is empty. It's hard work but I honestly feel it'll be worth the effort.

Edict 1

Get a fresh start

Chapter 2

Ed was enjoying his new-found freedom. Of the 92 people he emailed to let them know he was deleting all his messages, only 1 responded negatively. He decided it was definitely worth it.

He was talking to his co-worker, Mark, about it a couple of days later.

Hey Mark, how ya doin?

Can't complain. Even if I did, nobody would listen. I thought it was pretty cool what you did.

Yeah, thanks. I feel lighter now. Like a big weight has been kicked off my shoulders.

So how's it goin since the big day?

It's goin okay but I'm a little scared?

Why, did a lot of people complain?

No, not really, it's just that I'm not sure I can keep it from happening again. Mark, I've already got over a hundred messages in my Inbox and, although I really have been trying to deal with them as they come in, I'm already seeing a problem ahead. How about you, what do you do?

I use folders. I try to move what I can to folders and then I check them later.

That's what I've been doing but I've got like 47 folders already. Is that too many

No way, man, I've got over 100. The busier you are, the more folders you need.

On Thursday of the second week after Ed declared Email Emancipation, he had 61 folders and 327 messages in his Inbox. He was feeling better but not that much better. The elation from his first day of freedom had faded and he was starting to dread looking at his Inbox again.

He was thinking about these things as he drifted off to sleep that night.

In his dream, he found himself on the beach enjoying the sound of the waves and the wind. He was watching a little boy in a red bathing suit play with sand. For some reason he was drawn to the fact that the little boy was dumping sand out of one bucket and putting it into three smaller buckets.

After a while, the Email Angel sat down next to him.

How are you doing Ed?

Pretty good.

That little boy is the answer to the questions you were thinking about.

What do you mean?

The way he's moving the sand is the way you should move your emails.

Tell me more.

The problem with all your folders and lists is that you have to make sure to look at them at the right time. Although it's better than having them all in your Inbox, you have to remember to check them. You are human and so sometimes you forget. Also, it adds stress to have to remember and prioritize everything.

Ed, the first thing you need to do is put all the messages that you need to keep but that don't require action into one folder called **Reference***.*

But how will I find the messages?

Ed, how often do you need to find a message?

Not very often.

Also, you can use Desktop Search to find the ones you do need. It's much better than looking through folders. Get Randy, from the computer department, to install it for you.

Okay, so what are the other two buckets?

All of your other messages will be moved to Calendar or Tasks. Make sure you find the keyboard shortcut that will allow you to move the whole message including attachments to these places.

For items that have to be completed at a specific time, move them to Calendar.

For other items, move them to Tasks and assign them a due date. This due date can be either the precise deadline for which the item is actually due or a point in time where you want to look at that item again.

Anything else?

No. That's it for today.

Who's going to win the World Series?

That's not my department.

Thanks so much for your help.

Ed went to work the next day and began organizing his messages as the angel suggested. At first, it was hard and even awkward. His program required him to right-click and drag to move messages to Calendar or Tasks. He was surprised when, in about a week, he was actually starting to like this new system *and* he was missing fewer appointments and deadlines.

He thought, "I guess the angel really does know what he's talking about".

Edict 2

Use fewer folders for faster filing and retrieval

Chapter 3

About a month later things were going pretty well for Ed. He was feeling pretty good and people were starting to notice that his new email habits were making him easier to deal with.

On the other hand, he could never seem to get his Inbox to less than a couple of hundred messages. He knew this was way better than when he started (at over 4000 messages) but the problems of Email Hell were still constantly nagging at him. Could he do better?

On his way to lunch, he ran into Sharon who worked in another department. They started talking . . .

Well Ed, Mark told me that you are doing better with your email. Frankly, old buddy, you couldn't have done much worse. Just kidding. So how is it going?

It's going pretty well. I wish I could do better but I can never seem to get my Email Box from Hell all the way to empty.

Empty? If your Inbox is always empty people are going to think you're weird. They might even think you don't have enough to do. Having at least 50 or 60 messages in your Inbox makes you look busy and that's a good thing when it comes to resume enhancement. As always, there's talk of budget cuts. You don't want to give anybody the impression you don't have enough to do.

Well, Sharon, you've probably right. It just feels unfinished not to have the Inbox empty.

You know what they say, though, "A clean desk is a sign of a sick mind.".

I don't think I'm in any danger of that.

Have a good one, Sharon.

See ya, Ed

After Ed arrived home early that evening, he decided to go for a walk in the park near his place. He walked for a while, enjoying the cool breeze, the trees, and the sound of the birds. He sat down on the bench near the fountain to rest a bit. He looked to the right and saw some kids playing. Out of the corner of his eye he noticed someone coming over to sit on the bench next to him. It was the email angel wearing jeans!

Man, you are kinda freaking me out.

Fear not.

You guys like to say that.

I say what I say. How are things going with your email?

Pretty well.

Want to do better?

I guess.

I heard what Sharon said and she's wrong. You can do better.

Okay I'll buy that, Tell me how.

The next step for you is to empty your Inbox every time you open it.

Yeah, right. I mean, that may be possible where YOU work but not down here.

Sure it is. It's actually very simple. Don't even look at your emails unless you plan to go through every one and deal with them until your Inbox is empty.

Isn't that going to suck up too much of my time?

Try it and see. You will find great satisfaction and greater productivity if you do.

Okay, I'll try it. And by the way: Thanks, this is really helping me. I wish I had known all of this a couple of years ago.

You are welcome Ed. I will see you again when it's time.

The next day, Ed turned his phone off and slogged through all of his emails. After 7 grueling hours and 4 cups of high octane coffee, his Inbox was completely empty. Ed rocked back in his chair, threw both hands into the air and howled "yes!!" A couple of heads gophered above their cube walls and then everyone went back to working.

Over the next two weeks, Ed really made an effort to empty his Inbox every time he touched it. After a while, the process became second nature: it was just what he did.

Edict 3

Empty your Inbox
Every Time

Chapter 4

Things had been cruising along nicely for Ed. His new-found email organizational skills proved to be highly effective and people were starting to take notice. In fact, Ed had received a promotion! The promotion came with an extra bonus: a Blackberry.

The first few weeks after the big change he felt like a genuine big shot. Pretty soon, though, that old familiar feeling of being overwhelmed started creeping back in around his happy edges. Thanks to his new position, his Email Inbox from Hell was expanding than ever before. And that really cool Blackberry? It was starting to feel more like a curse than a blessing. Sure it was nice to be able to send an email from anywhere. It was also great to have his calendar and contacts with him wherever he was. On the other hand, the thing seemed to never quit buzzing. One time, it even woke him up at midnight buzzing because of some stupid appointment reminder. Yuk!

About a month after he first fired up his Blackberry, Ed was driving home from the office and the Email angel suddenly popped into the passenger's seat.

Angel, you scared me.

Fear not. Ed, what are you doing?

Typing an email on my Blackberry.

Do you think that's wise while controlling a half ton vehicle moving at these speeds?

Everybody does it.

Do you remember what your mother said about that?

Okay, point taken. Why are you here?

I'm here to give you two rules that will bring your Blackberry into balance.

Okay, I'm ready to hear it. This thing is driving me crazy.

Rule 1: Turn off all notifications but the phone. Otherwise it interrupts you way too often.

Rule 2: Look at the screens no more than once an hour.

Do you think that will help or should I just get rid of it?

If you follow those rules, your Blackberry will be a blessing and not a curse.

Sure enough, Ed followed the Email angel's instructions and in a couple of weeks he was loving his Blackberry. It was proving to be a great help in the journey toward his personal escape from Email Hell.

Edict 4: Turn off all email notifications

Chapter 5

About 9 months after his first visit from the Email Angel, Ed had a dream. In the dream he woke up on a keyboard about the size of a city block.

Hello Ed, how are you?

Hello, Angel, I'm doing well. Why am I here?

You are here to learn how to do things even faster in your email.

I guess this may have something to do with the keyboard.

You know, Ed, you're turning out to be much smarter than you look. Years ago, a company called Palm Computing ruled the hand held computer market. Part of the reason for this was the simplicity of their devices. At Palm, there was a guy who was called the "Click Counter." He had a very important job: Make sure that any user could do anything on the Palm in 4 clicks or less. You, Edward, need to become your own "Click Counter."

You are doing well with your Email but you still rely on the mouse and the menus way too much. Taking some time out to learn the keyboard shortcuts can save you a lot of time. For instance, did you know that many times the keyboard shortcuts are 3 or 4 times faster than other methods? Think about the time savings in managing over 100, or even 1,000, messages.

Okay, Angel, I'll buy that but how do I learn these processes? Are you going to tell me?

I could tell you but its better if you uncover them yourself. The best place to begin your journey is by looking in the Help menu.

Ed, one more thing, as you find shortcuts that you like, learn them one at a time. Put a note on your screen that steps you through the shortcuts and take it down when you have all the details memorized.

Thanks, Angel, I'll try it.

Edict 5: Find the fastest way and use it

Chapter 6

Well things were going along pretty well for Ed. His email-related stress was becoming less and less of a problem. In fact, he was pretty satisfied with his email at work. On the other hand he was noticing that his home emails were really piling up—Email Hell had found him again. On the home front, Ed was using three different webmail services and the real world inter-connections were not very smooth.

One night as Ed sat on his couch trudging through his complex web of email purgatory, the Email Angel appeared, lounging at the other end. Ed was so startled that he just about dumped his laptop on the floor.

How are you Ed?

I'm doing okay, angel. How about you?

In heaven things are always good. I was watching you stumble through your email when I decided I needed to make another visit. Would you like to make this chore a little smoother?

Sure.

Ed, what you need to do is use the right tool. That tool needs to be available both offline and online. In addition, you need to be able to move your messages to folders, calendars, and tasks. Guess what, Ed; you are using the right tool at work. You just need to use one like it at home too.

But I like my webmail.

Don't worry, you can still use webmail when you have to, but it will be so much better if you use the same tool most of the time. It's much easier to use the same shortcuts and techniques at home as you use at work.

Okay, I see your point. Tell me more.

This weekend, pick up a copy of the software like you use at work and install it on your laptop. Then have Carol help you set it up so that all three of your webmail accounts are automatically pulled to your single desktop email client.

Once that's done, you can manage your home email just like you manage your email at work. You'll be surprised at how much faster it is.

Thanks, Angel.

So Ed did as the Angel suggested and he was really surprised at how much better things went. One immediate benefit was that he no longer had to login to three different email accounts. And the Angel was right; it was easier when he used one application all the time for all of his email. He thought he'd miss those webmail applications but he found he didn't. On the other hand, he could still use them every now and then when he didn't have access to his own computer.

Things were just getting better and better for Ed.

Edict 6: Manage all your email using one tool

Chapter 7

One Friday, a little over a year after his first visit from the Email Angel, Ed receives a message from his boss: "Come see me right away." Ed was worried but went to see her anyway.

Ed, the company has noticed your increase in productivity and we've decided to offer you another promotion. Now, before you make a decision, I want to tell you a little more about it. About 50% of the time you would be traveling to other locations. Oh course; we would give you a laptop and a corporate credit card. If you accept the position, we'll also give you an immediate 15% pay increase. Even better, you will now be eligible for quarterly performance bonuses.

Are you interested?

Ed didn't even have to think about it. "Yes," he blurted, "I would like the job."

Great, I'll finish the paperwork, and you can start your new work on Monday. I know you've documented your current position and that Doug is cross-trained for your duties as well. From time to time he may have questions but he has already agreed to accept your old job.

That night, Ed was heading to the parking deck. He was so excited he was whistling! He rounded the corner and saw his car and . . . there was someone in the front seat. It was the Email Angel.

Hi, Ed. Congratulations on your new job.

Thanks, I wouldn't have gotten it without you. In fact, I might have been fired.

Ed, unlike others I have tried to help, you have actually done what I've suggested.

Thanks.

I have another suggestion for you: ask your boss on Monday to let you put your personal emails on your new laptop.

Okay, I'll do it.

And with that the Email Angel vanished.

On the following Monday Ed asked his boss about managing his personal emails on his work laptop and she said yes. On the other hand, she also said that any problems caused by spyware and viruses coming from his personal emails would be his responsibility.

At lunch, Ed was thinking about how bad it could be if a virus from his email spread to the rest of the company. He was starting to reconsider the Angel's advice when he noticed a memo on his desk. It was from the Email Angel. Now, that was a new one.

By now, you've talked to your boss and she has said yes. Also, she has told you that any problems caused by your personal email would be your responsibility. Here is how we are going to handle that.

1. *Use a hosted Exchange Mail Box to consolidate your work and home email. Ask George, your friend from church, about this. He is already using a good service. With this service all your email will be pulled into a single mailbox you can access from anywhere you have an internet connection.*
2. *Use a service to filter out all your SPAM. Having a person filter out your SPAM not only saves you time but it also lessens the chance of Spyware infection.*

Both of these services will cost you some money but you can afford it with your new raise.

Well, it took Ed a little time and a little money to get it all set up, but it was worth it. With his new process in place, he didn't get any SPAM and all his messages ended up in the same place. Everything worked great.

Edict 7: Use services to consolidate and filter your email

Chapter 8

Ed's new job was going well. The travel was an adjustment but he was home every other week. And besides, he got to keep all his frequent flyer miles!

It was really cool getting all his messages on his laptop, especially since he didn't have to waste time filtering out SPAM. Sometimes, though, it was distracting to see his personal emails popping up on his work computer. And it was no fun being reminded of work when he was "off the clock." That night he had a dream.

In the dream he was in the back office of a large post office. He was fascinated with how quickly the mail was sorted into the different locations automatically.

Hello, Ed.

Hello, Angel.

Ed, you need to automate your email processing. Here's what you need to do. Set up rules so that every message goes to one of four folders: Inbox (for key people), Home, Work, and Unknown (those not in your address book).

That sounds good. That way I would only look at Work messages while I'm at work and Home messages while I'm at home.

That's the idea Ed.

So with a little help from the Help Desk, Ed got his rules set up. After that things went much more smoothly.

Edict 8: Use rules to automate your email processing

Chapter 9

Well, Ed had been in his new job for about 2 months. He was doing well but found he wanted to create more blocks of open time where he could work on important projects without interruption.

He was listening to the in-flight radio on a long flight to Seattle when he heard a familiar voice.

Hello, Angel, he thought.

Ed, since you've got some time on this flight, I thought I could tell you how you can get more uninterrupted time to work on your special projects.

What you need to do is establish a schedule for checking your email and only check it according to that schedule. I suggest that you check those messages from your key contacts (the ones that show up in your Inbox) once an hour. Check your Work folder at 10 and 2 and check your Home folder once at night. For those in your Unknown folder, I suggest you check them once a day.

All you have to do to accomplish this is *to set up some auto-responders to reply to everyone but your key contacts. For each one, just let them know when you plan to check your email. For instance, for Work you might say, "I check my email each day at 10 and 2 and will respond to your email at that time".*

Since you have a little time, why don't you go ahead and set up those auto-responders now.

So Ed got his laptop out of the overhead and set up the auto-responders.

When he first started checking his email only once an hour, it was hard. He didn't realize how often he was checking his email. But after a while he settled into his new habit. Pretty soon, he was enjoying regular hour-long blocks of time where he could concentrate on his emails. Life was getting better and better for Ed.

Edict 9: Only check your email when you plan to

Chapter 10

Well, Ed was feeling pretty smug about life these days and downright great about his email. Lately, his visits from the Email Angel had been focused more on writing better emails rather than about his email management. As Ed began writing better emails he found that he was getting better emails in return. What had Ed learned about writing better emails?

Never use email for negative communication. Ed found that correcting someone or addressing any other negative issues just didn't work well in Emails. Negative emailing led to hurt feelings and that people tended to read those emails again and again and--even passing them along to others. Instead, Ed learned to pick up the phone or schedule a meeting for touchy subjects.

Create better subject lines. Ed's goal was to create a subject line that would allow the recipient to easily prioritize messages from him without ever opening them. For Ed, a good subject line included three things: the purpose of the message, the action requested, and when a response was expected. For example, "Need Your Input on Survey (Please respond by 10/5)."

Include multiple options. Sometimes it seemed like scheduling a meeting with someone required a dozen or more messages. Ed would suggest a time and then the email exchanges would commence. He couldn't free time up for the first scheduled time, so he would suggest an alternative and so on. So Ed started including multiple options in the first email. Something like, "Would Tuesday at 10, Wednesday at 2:30, or Thursday for lunch be better for you?"

Use templates for common responses. For common responses Ed developed some templates where he could just fill in the blanks and send the message. These worked great.

Things had changed so much for Ed. He had been thinking about quitting his job but instead received a promotion. Now, his co-workers were calling him "Ed the Email Guy". Ed had escaped from Email Hell and moved into Email Heaven.

Edict 10: Write better emails to get better responses

Closing

Well, give yourself a round of applause. You made it! I trust that you have taken some of these ideas and made them your own. I hope they have made a significant difference in the way you manage your email. As your life changes, I encourage you to revisit the ideas. They will serve you well in whatever role you find for yourself.

This book is one man's opinion on what works. I would love to hear from you about what works in your specific environment. To find my current contact information, visit my website http://www.craighuggart.com/ and check my LinkedIn information.

I look forward to hearing from you and maybe meeting you in person as time goes on.

May you find your way out of Email Hell and into Email Heaven!

Appendix 1 – My Favorite Outlook Shortcuts[1]

Chapter 1

- The keyboard shortcut for creating a new folder is **CTRL+SHIFT+E**

- To move all your messages, select all of them using **CTRL+A**, and then click and drag the messages to the folder you want them in.

Chapter 2

- To move message to a folder, click the **Move to Folder** button (with the message open) and select the folder you want to move the message to.

- To move a message to the Calendar or to the Task list the procedure is the same.

  o Right-click the envelope icon, click and drag the message to either the Calendar or Task icon.

  o Drop the message on the icon and choose either *Move Here as Appointment with Attachment* (Calendar) or *Move Here as Task with Attachment* (Tasks).

---

[1] These shortcuts have been tested in Outlook 2007 and Outlook 2003. Most will work in earlier versions as well.

Other Chapters

Task	Shortcut
Create a New Message	CTRL+SHIFT+M
Delete Message	CTRL+D
Forward Message	CTRL+F
Mark as Read	CTRL+Q
Mark as Unread	CTRL+U
Next Message	CTRL+Comma
Previous Message	CTRL+Period
Reply	CTRL+R
Print	CTRL+P
Save	CTRL+S
Send	ALT+S

The 10 Edicts for Escaping Email Hell

Edict 1: Get a fresh start

Edict 2: Use fewer folders for faster filing and retrieval

Edict 3: Empty your Inbox Every Time

Edict 4: Turn off all email notifications

Edict 5: Find the fastest way and use it

Edict 6: Manage all your email using one tool

Edict 7: Use services to consolidate and filter your email

Edict 8: Use rules to automate your email processing

Edict 9: Only check your email when you plan to

Edict 10: Write better emails to get better response

www.ingramcontent.com/pod-product-compliance
Lightning Source LLC
Chambersburg PA
CBHW051213050326
40689CB00008B/1299